AURORA
A Tale of the Northern Lights

By MINDY DWYER

ALASKA NORTHWEST BOOKS™

Anchorage   Seattle   Portland

*E*arly one morning in a long ago northern land, a baby girl was born. Her mother named her Aurora, which means the "rosy light of dawn." This faraway place knew only a daylight sky, for the sun would glide from one end of the sky to the other, hugging the horizon but never slipping below. As each day passed, only the changing colors of the sky—from shimmering blue to an eerie green to the softest pink— would signal the time of day.

Carpets of tundra filled with delicate wildflowers stretched as far as the eye could see in this land without darkness. Caribou lived alongside Aurora and her people.

Each year the caribou gathered into great herds and traveled an old familiar path to a mysterious midnight place, later returning to their home of light and flowers.

Aurora grew into a dreamy young girl, curious about what lay beyond the distant horizon. She wondered where the caribou went and often daydreamed of traveling with the herds, prancing across the tundra.

Under the pink glow of an early morning sun, Aurora spotted a lone caribou. How strange that he was not with his herd, she thought. At first, she followed him, watching as the caribou playfully kicked up his hooves.

Then, Aurora ran and the caribou ran, frolicking together across the tundra in a magnificent dance.

*B*efore she knew it, Aurora was in the open tundra, far from her family. Feeling adventurous, she was ready to walk the way of the caribou.

Soon Aurora grew hungry. Deep in the purple
shadows, she found some blueberries. She plopped
to the ground to rest and enjoy their sweet taste.
The velvety blue color of the berries reminded
Aurora of a story Grandmother told of a place
where darkness fell each night and the sky turned
a deep and peaceful indigo. How she longed to
see this for herself.

As Aurora continued her journey across the soft, green tundra, she was comforted by the memory of her favorite grandmother. Grandmother's gentle voice told once more of the dark sky Aurora had never seen:

In the dark times, the sky wrapped itself around us.
Inside each one of us, there is a glow that lights the way.
It keeps us warm and we are not afraid.

Grandmother's words were a mystery to her. Aurora felt sure she would understand them when she arrived in the land where darkness fell and where the sky turned the color of ripe blueberries.

The caribou continued to lead Aurora in her long journey from home. To be safe and warm in the dark place, Aurora began to collect the colors from the daylight sky.

As days passed, Aurora gathered the

delicate pink morning light and put it in her pocket.

The midday light
was a shining silver
blue, and this she
placed in her pocket, too.

Twilight glowed a luminous green. This was Aurora's favorite time of day, and she filled her pockets with its color. She walked, then danced with the changing colors of the sky.

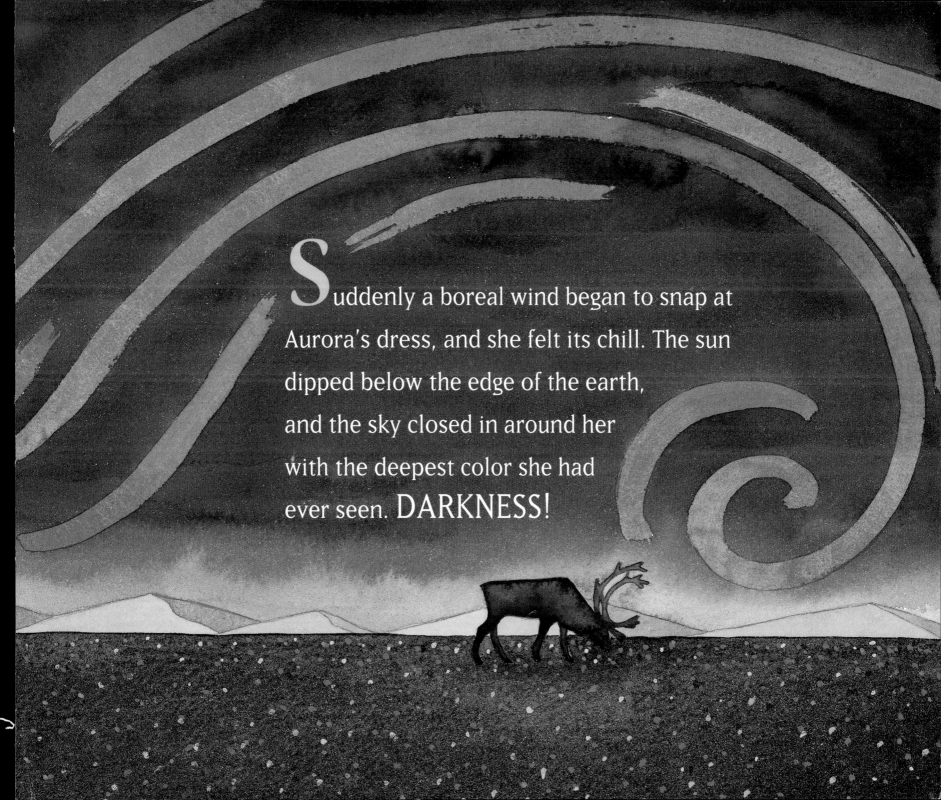

Suddenly a boreal wind began to snap at Aurora's dress, and she felt its chill. The sun dipped below the edge of the earth, and the sky closed in around her with the deepest color she had ever seen. DARKNESS!

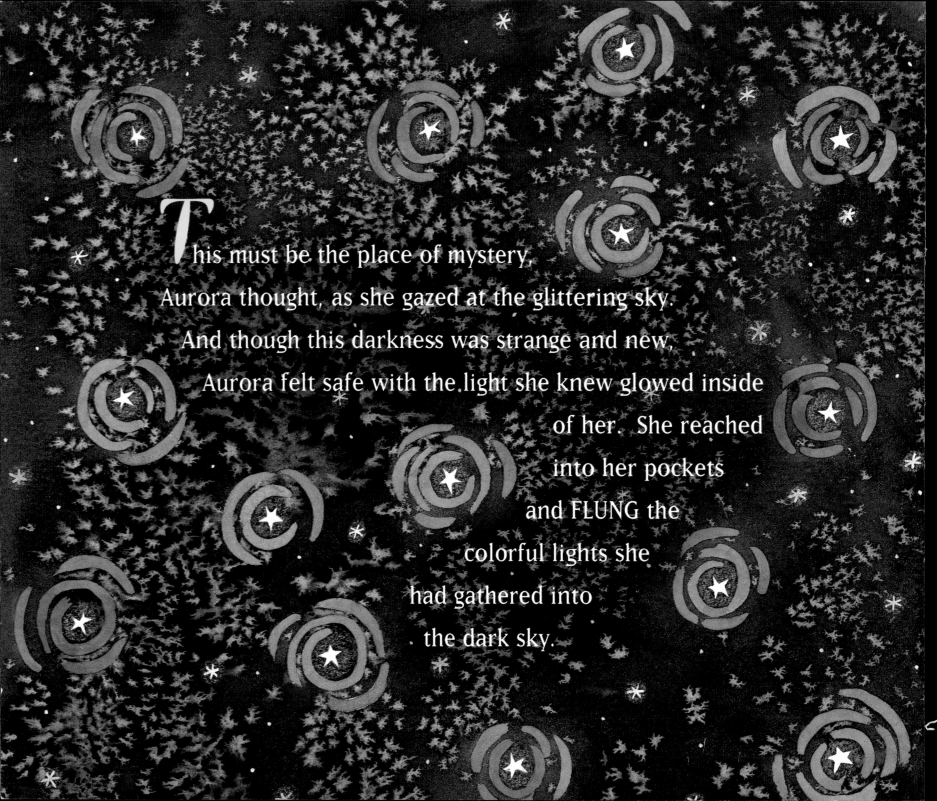

*T*his must be the place of mystery,

Aurora thought, as she gazed at the glittering sky.

And though this darkness was strange and new,

Aurora felt safe with the light she knew glowed inside

of her. She reached

into her pockets

and FLUNG the

colorful lights she

had gathered into

the dark sky.

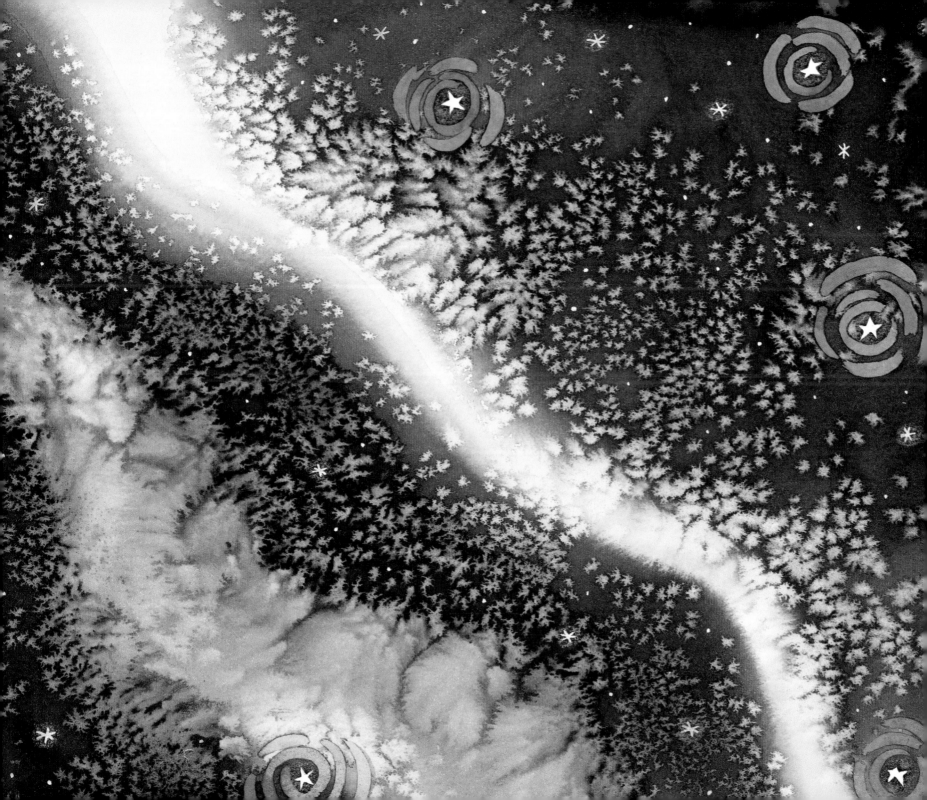

Aurora played with the lights, admiring the way they danced across the sky, just as she had danced across the tundra with the lone caribou. The lights grew ever brighter, shimmering like a curtain of color in the darkness. Aurora's family saw the dancing lights and followed, hoping they would find their beloved daughter.

Although she had brought the colors of the daylight sky to comfort her, Aurora found that she was not afraid in the dark place of the indigo sky. She now understood Grandmother's mysterious words.

Together again, Aurora and her family celebrated her journey with the caribou, which had led Aurora to discover courage and her own inner light.

The adventurous spirit of Aurora lives on. When you gaze into the night sky of the North and see the dancing lights, you are watching Aurora's many colors, collected on her special journey long ago.

GLOSSARY

The northern lands seem

to be full of magic. While

the events of this story are

imaginary, there are many

aspects that are very real.

These are just a few:

ARCTIC CIRCLE: circle of latitude at 66 1/2 degrees, marking the southernmost point where the sun can be seen for a full 24-hour period.

AURORA BOREALIS: streams of colored light—shades of green, blue, white, purple—that shimmer in the dark night sky of the earth's polar regions. Also called Northern Lights.

BOREAL WIND: a cold north wind.

CARIBOU: a large deer of northern North America related to the reindeer, having large palmate antlers (meaning that they spread outward as fingers on a hand), broad flat hooves, a heavy double coat, short ears and tail.

MIDNIGHT SUN: 24 hours of daylight occurring at the polar regions, above the arctic circle.

SUMMER SOLSTICE: a day around June 22, the first day of summer and the longest day of the year, when the sun is closest to the northern hemisphere of the earth.

TUNDRA: a level treeless plain found in the Arctic, with permanently frozen ground covered by black, mucky soil. Plants are dwarfed, but mosses and lichens grow thickly, and there are many miniature wildflowers.

Library of Congress Cataloging-in-Publication Data:

Dwyer, Mindy, 1957-
    Aurora : a tale of the Northern Lights / by Mindy Dwyer.
        p.   cm.
    Summary: After getting lost while following a caribou, a
young girl sets off across the Arctic tundra gathering the
colors of the sky which become the Northern Lights.
    ISBN 0-88240-494-6
    [1. Aurora—Fiction. 2. Arctic regions—Fiction.]   I. Title.
    PZ7.09635Au   1997
    [E]—dc21
                                                    97-11295
                                                       CIP
                                                       AC

Editors: Marlene Blessing, Ellen Wheat
Designer: Elizabeth Watson

Alaska Northwest Books™
An imprint of Graphic Arts Center Publishing Company
P.O. Box 10306, Portland, OR 97210
Catalogs and book orders: 800-452-3032

Printed in Canada

Dedicated to Bill, who brought me to Alaska